Travel stories for

intermediate English

students

Rhys Joseph

Rhys Joseph

rhysbjj@gmail.com

I hope you enjoy this book and it helps you learn more English.

Check out study and learn English on Instagram, and our website, for more English help.

www.instagram.com/study_and_learn_english/

www.study-and-learn-english.com

If you enjoy this book, please give it a positive reference

so other students can find it more easily online, thanks.

These short stories are designed for English students with an intermediate level of English who want to improve their grammar, vocabulary, and reading comprehension in English

Lower-Intermediate & Intermediate students

B1 & B2 level Cambridge exams: The 1st Certificate

IELTS EXAM 4.0 – 5.0

PET EXAM

BED PRELIMINARY

If you are studying English for one of these exams, or you have passed one of these exams, then these short travel stories are for your current level of English.

The stories will include some difficult vocabulary, which will be **highlighted** and underlined in the story and explained at the end of each chapter. The stories will also include some simple, but important phrasal verbs and these will also be **highlighted** and underlined in the text for you to review at the end of each chapter.

Each chapter will also have a small summary at the end, so you can check to see if you have understood what is happening in Each chapter.

Very descriptive words will also be marked like this, *****, in the vocabulary list. At the end of the book you will find example sentences with these words. For example;

Chapter Summary

In this chapter many things happened and here you will see a summary of the story. Here you can check to see if you have understood the chapter.......

Vocabulary

Here the difficult words from each chapter are explained to help you understand the story……...

Highlighted – to make something more clear or more obvious ****

Underlined – to make a line under a word to make it more clear

Word - explanation

Word - explanation

Review – an assessment or appraisal of something ****

Final Vocabulary Review

You will find the final vocabulary review at the end of each story. Here you will find the most difficult or useful words explained with some examples……..

Highlighted – to make something more clear or more obvious

- he highlighted a problem with the report
- We need to highlight this for our boss

Review – an assessment or appraisal of something

- Somebody reviewed the film and said it was very good

So, if you are ready, let's get started!

Story One – A Camper Van Adventure in Australia

Chapter One

John had just finished high school and didn't know what to do with his life. He was 18 and his parents had told him that he should go to university, but that is not what he really wanted to do. What John really wanted to do was to travel around the world and see lots of things. He was really **keen** to see the world.

John arrived in Australia from England in early October. It was a long flight, he stopped in Dubai and Kuala Lumpur along the way and the whole trip took about 32 hours. After arriving in Sydney, he did not really know what to do. He knew he wanted to travel, but he didn't have any plans, so he spent a couple of weeks **hanging out at a** few different hostels and seeing tourist sites.

John knew he wanted to see Australia, and maybe more places, but he really didn't have a plan or know where he wanted to go or how he was going to get there. He had thought about **hitch-hiking** around, but he had never done that before and he wasn't sure if it was going to be possible. He had spent the summer working different jobs in England to **save up** enough money to travel and pay for his flights, so he had enough money for about 6 months he thought.

Back in England he had done several different jobs and none of them were much fun, but they had been a good way to **put together** some money. He had worked for a couple of months with a **removals company**, and that had been really tough. The company specialized in moving large companies into new offices, so they spent all day carrying heavy boxes up and downstairs. Up and down, up and down and up and down again. It was an **exhausting** job and he had only lasted for a short time.

Apart from that he had worked at a magazine **factory**. The **shifts** ran from 6 in the afternoon to 6 in the morning, all night long, with only 30 minutes for a break. This was difficult to **get used to**, but the hours were convenient because John could **borrow** his mother's car after she came home from work, and then he would arrive home in the morning before she needed to use it again, so the hours were convenient. The factory printed all the magazine pages and then put them, all into a huge machine to put them together into a completed magazine. John spent all night carrying **stacks** of magazines and carrying them from one to another.

John had done several other jobs like this, in factories and other similar places. None of the jobs were fun, but over several months he had **saved up** enough money to buy his plane ticket to Australia for his big adventure. And now he was here in Sydney, so excited to start his adventure, but without any idea what to do next.

That was when he met Tim and Ben....

Chapter Summary

*check to see if you understood the chapter

John really wants to have an adventure. He saves up money in England by doing several different jobs. The jobs are not nice, but he works hard and saves some money and goes to Australia to start his adventure. When he arrives in Australia he does not know what to do and spends some time at different hostels, and visiting tourist sites. He then meets two new people, Ben and Tim.

Vocabulary

Keen – excited, enthusiastic, eager to do something: ardent, eager
****

Hang out – loiter, spend time, wait around doing nothing in particular ****

Hitch-hike – to travel by asking people to go in their car

Save up – to keep and store money for future use

Put together – same meaning as save up here

Removals company - a company which helps people move their things to a new hour or office

Exhausting – very tiring: draining, taxing, tiresome

Factory - an industrial space where things are produced

Shift – the time you work, night shift or day shift

Get used to – to become accustomed to, habituated to ****

Borrow - to use something belonging to another person and later return it

Stacks – a large quantity of something, a pile of, papers, boxes, magazines

Chapter Two

Tim and Ben were two surfers from the south of England. They had gone to Australia with the dream of travelling around and surfing all the best beaches. They had also worked in England to **save up** enough money for their dream trip. They planned to buy a **camper van** so they could travel all around Australia, which is a big place, and visit all the beaches they had always dreamed of seeing.

John met Ben and Tim when they were staying in the same hostel and they became friends. They began talking and quickly all realized that they had the same interests and started to visit some tourist places together. Tim and Ben were surfing almost every day, they had brought their surfboards with them from England. They started to teach John how to surf because he had **grown up** in a place far away from the sea and, unlike them, he had never surfed before in his life.

After **getting to know** each other for a week or two, Tim and Ben decided to tell John about their plan to buy a camper van and travel all around Australia and invited him to join them on the adventure. John was so excited to be invited along on this amazing adventure and was very happy to accept the invitation and join them. Now he had a plan for his trip and knew what he wanted to do. He was going to explore Australia with Tim and Ben, learn to surf, and see amazing places and things. He was **over the moon!**

The three new friends started looking for a campervan to buy together. They **worked out** how much money they had and decided how much they could afford to spend on the camper van and started looking around. They started looking in the local newspapers and asking people where they could find a cheap camper van. They didn't have a lot of money, but if the three of them put their money together they could **afford** something that should be ok for the adventure they planned.

After a couple of weeks of searching, they found what they were looking for. The camper van was old and a little dirty. The owner was an old man who had been the owner of the camper van for a long time and now he wanted to sell it. The old man hadn't used the camper van for at least a year, and it had been sitting parked in front of his house getting **rusty**. The three friends knew that this was a good opportunity to buy a camper van cheaply, and they thought that with a little work, and some cleaning, it would be nice and new again soon. They offered the man a small amount of money for the van, and he accepted. They had a camper van for their adventure!

Chapter Summary

John Met his new friends, Ben and Tim, in Australia. They decided to buy a campervan together to travel around Australia and surf. They looked for, and found, a cheap campervan and bought it. Now their adventure could begin.

Vocabulary

Save up - To work to collect or accumulate money

Campervan - A vehicle that is it possible to sleep in, with a small kitchen and bed

Grow up - When a person gets older, different from grow.

Get to know - We use to *get to know* for new people or places ****

Over the moon - An expression to English to *very happy*: delighted, elated, joyful

Work out - To calculate something ****

Afford - To be able to pay for, or do, something: allow, manage ****

Rusty - When metal gets old and wet, it rusts: oxidized, decayed

Chapter Three

The three friends spent a couple of weeks tidying up their new camper van and getting everything together. They bought a map and discussed where to go first. Was it North or South, East or West?

In the end, they based the plan on Ben and Tim's dream beaches, most of which were to the South. So they **set out** on the trip on a **sunny** Thursday morning and began their journey south. The trip went really well and they were having a great time, visiting beaches, surfing every day. John was having a great time and learning to surf. They discovered that there were lots of places in Australia you could just stop at the side of the road, near a beach, and it was a great place to camp or to sleep in the campervan. There were even free BBQ places at some beaches, with a little roof over a gas-powered BBQ. You only had to press a button and the BBQ would work for 20 minutes and you could cook food that you bought in the supermarket. Can you imagine ever seeing something like that back in **rainy** England? A free BBQ for people camping at the beach, they couldn't believe it and they thought they were in paradise!

The trip continued like this for several weeks, surfing every day and visiting new places. They reached the state of Victoria, more to the south of Australia and drove along the famous Great Ocean Road. One day they went surfing at an amazing beach, and it started to rain as they were in the water, but it was still warm and it felt great. They were all a little worried about sharks because there are so many in Australia and there are not really any back in England. John was especially scared of sharks, and he was also not really **used to** being in the ocean every day. The other two were used to surfing a lot and being in the ocean.

One day, back in Sydney before he had met Tim and Ben, John had been swimming at a beach. He was not in very **deep** water and he was having a great time. **Suddenly**, from **underneath** him in the water, a huge dark black shape **came up towards** his legs. He could see a big black shape with a **fin** in the water underneath him! He was certain it was a shark and he was about to be **bitten**, maybe even killed. It was the scariest moment of his life. He was so scared that he **froze** in the water and started to **sink**! His head went under the water but he was so scared he could not move any part of his party as he continued to sink! But it wasn't a shark, he was very lucky, it was a dolphin! It swam past him and he saw it in the water before it disappeared. He recovered and swam back to the beach, so happy that it had only been a dolphin. After that time, he was always really scared of sharks, **whenever** he was in the water.

Anyway, they didn't see any sharks in Victoria, or when they stopped to see the beaches along the Great Ocean Road, and the trip continued. They were all really happy, in fact, John thought it was the happiest he had ever been in his whole life. This was exactly what he had always wanted. Adventure!

Chapter Summary

The adventure holiday was going very well and the three friends were having a great time. John was scared of sharks because he had a bad experience with a dolphin before, but the trip was really fun.

Vocabulary

Set out - To begin a journey or trip

Sunny - When there's a lot of sun, it is sunny

Rainy - When there's a lot of rain, it is rainy

Used to - To be accustomed to

Deep - When there is a lot of water, the opposite of shallow

Suddenly - When something happens quickly, in an unexpected way: abruptly, quickly, swiftly ****

Underneath - A preposition, meaning under: lower, beneath

Come up towards - To approach from underneath

Fin - The triangular shape on the back of a shark or dolphin

Bitten - Bite, bit, bitten. A dog can bite you, like a shark

Scary - When a situation makes you afraid or scared, it is a scary situation:alarming, chilling, shocking ****

Freeze - When something is very cold, it can freeze. You can also freeze when you are very scared

Whenever - Any time something happens, at any given moment ****

Chapter Four

The adventure continued and they reached the south of Australia. They were not spending too much money and they calculated that they would have enough money to continue for some more time. The one important thing was that they needed to try and sell the campervan after they finished their trip to **get some money back**. They had each invested some money into the campervan and hoped to get some of it back at the end. Tim especially wanted to try and get some money back because he planned to continue to New

Zealand after they all finished their trip to Australia. He wanted to continue and surf there as well, but he didn't have a lot of money and he always said he needed to try and get his part of the money back when they sold the camper van.

It wasn't a **luxurious** camper van, but for the three of them, it was good. In truth, it wasn't really a campervan at all. A real campervan is something professional, with beds, a shower, a kitchen, tables and chairs, a place where you can travel and live in comfort. The van that the three friends had bought was just a simple van that they put a **mattress** into the back of to sleep on. Three of them slept on the mattress every night, and every night they changed position because the person that slept on the left side, next to the door had the most **uncomfortable** position, so they **rotated** every night.

But **although** it wasn't luxurious, for them it was fantastic and they had a great time. When they **reached** the south of Australia they looked at a map, calculated how much money that had and made a plan. They had now spent 2 months in the van and it had been fantastic. What they planned to do was to travel through the south of Australia and then drive all the way over to the west of Australia.

This was a big **long drive** across the desert, several days, and they needed to be sure that the van would not **break down** during this trip. On that desert road, there were hundreds of miles when you did not see another car or any place to stop and get **fuel.**

The plan was to travel to a city in the south of Australia called Adelaide where they would spend some time making **repairs** to the van and checking that everything was in good condition to make the long drive to the west. They would maybe buy some **spare** parts **in case** the van broke down in the middle of the desert. They knew that if they arrived in Western Australia, a city called Perth, they could sell the van for much more money over there. Most people did not drive all the way to Perth, so the van would be **worth** much more money there. It was a perfect plan, and it was going to be their biggest adventure yet. They were really excited!

Chapter Summary

The three friends arrived in the south of Australia on their trip and decided they wanted to continue to the West of Australia, which was far away. They wanted to sell the campervan there to get some money to continue travelling.

Vocabulary

Get money back - to have money return and manage to take your money again

Luxurious - a very elegant, luxury, expensive, or high-quality item: opulent, deluxe, palatial

Mattress - the soft thing you sleep on, on your bed

Uncomfortable - not comfortable: difficult, hard, annoying ****

Rotate - to spin around: pivot, revolve, twirl

Although - a modal verb to contrast: albeit, despite, even if, though ****

Reached - to arrive at a place

Long drive - a big trip in the car

Breakdown - when the car stops working

Fuel - the fluid that makes the car work: combustible, gas, juice

Repairs - to fix something: improvement, overhaul, mend

Spare - an extra of something: unused, backup, free

In case - contingent upon, given, if, subject to

Worth - the value of something: cost, price, rate

Chapter Five

The three friends spent some time in Adelaide preparing their trip. They visited some tourist places in the city and had a good time, and they bought some spare parts for the van and generally made preparations. After about one week they decided they were ready for the big trip to the West of Australia.

They were a little nervous because they knew it was going to be a **risky** trip. It was almost 2000 miles in total, nearly 3,000 km. It was a long way. They thought it would be about 30 hours of driving in total, so maybe 5-6 days in their slow old van. Many people told them it was a little dangerous and they needed to be 100% sure that their vehicle was strong and would not **break down**. They needed to take lots of extra water and fuel.

The truth is that the three boys were not 100% sure about their car. They had already had one or two small mechanical problems on their trip. Nothing very serious, but for this big drive across the desert, they were a little nervous. They had a couple of problems when their engine got too hot on the trip and when the old van was not strong enough to drive up a big hill and they had to push! But they decided that they were going to try. It was risky, but it was going to be the biggest adventure of their lives, and if they really made it to Perth, in the west of Australia, it would be amazing!

The three friends decided that they had made all the preparations they could. They had lots of extra food, water and fuel for the car. They had bought some extra parts for the car and read a book about how to fix the most common problems that happen when the car gets too hot in the desert on the big drive. They decide that tomorrow they would spend one more day in Adelaide before starting the big risky adventure. They were going to visit a famous and beautiful beach to go surfing, and then they would go out to a restaurant for a big expensive dinner. The next day they would start the adventure and drive all the way across the desert to Perth. They were really excited!

Chapter Summary

The journey to Perth was a little dangerous and the three friends were not completely sure about the reliability of the campervan. They continued to make preparations.

Vocabulary

Risky - Something that involves risk or danger is risky

Break down - When a vehicle, or complicated mechanism breaks or stops working ****

Chapter Six

Tim, Ben and John woke up early the next morning to go to the beach. It was to be their final day in Adelaide before the big drive west and they were both excited and nervous. They organized their surf equipment and **set out** for the beach. That day they were going to visit a famous surf beach. But the beach was also famous for another reason – sharks!

The beach was famous for an **unpleasant** incident a few years previously, when a shark killed a man. It was a very sad story because the man had been on his honeymoon. He was standing in the water with his wife when the shark got him. The strange thing about the story is that the water was not deep, they had only been standing in water that came up to their waist. It was really not very deep. The shark swam into the bay and went into the **shallow** water. The strange thing about this story is that the shark attacked the man from the beach side. The shark swam around in a big circle behind the couple, who were standing in the shallow water, and it **grabbed** the man by the legs from behind and swam with him out into the deep water. Very sadly, the man died on his honeymoon. It became a famous story in Australia.

John was already nervous about sharks because of his experience with the dolphin when he was swimming in Sydney. But after travelling with Tim and Ben around Australia in their campervan, he now felt more confident. He had learned how to surf and he felt more comfortable in the water. But still, surfing on this famous beach, famous for a terrible reason, he was still nervous. People say that you should not be nervous about sharks because driving to the beach in your car is actually much more dangerous than the shark. You are much more **likely** to have a car accident than be attacked by a shark, but John was much more scared of sharks than his car so this idea did not really help him

In the end, the day was fantastic. Nothing happened, there were no sharks, and the surfing was really good. Even though John was nervous, he had a good time in the water and he was really happy and **relieved** when they finished surfing and he could go back to the beach to eat some food and enjoy the sun. Tim and Ben also had a great time surfing and enjoying the sun before their big drive the next day. They were not nervous about sharks anyway. They were always relaxed.

The three friends enjoyed some sun on the beach together, put all their surf stuff back into the van and prepared to drive back to the place where they were camping. They all got into the van, no shoes on and no t-shirts on, only beach shorts. The weather was warm and they were on a surf holiday. They all felt great, excited about their big drive the next day and also **looking forward to** going to a restaurant that night and spending some money on a big meal in celebration. Tim was driving the van that day, and he started the engine and they left the beach. It was a great day, but things were about to change.

Chapter Summary

The three friends went to a beach to surf. This beach had a bad reputation, but the day was nice and nothing bad happened.

Vocabulary

Set out - To begin or commence a journey or trip

Unpleasant - not nice: disagreeable, distasteful, nasty ****

Shallow - water which is not deep

Grab - to take hold of something: catch, clutch, grasp

Likely - probable to happen: expected, possible, prone

Relieved - happy something did not happen: relaxed, satisfied, alleviated

Looking forward to - happy about something happening in the future: anticipate, count on, hope ****

Chapter Seven

Making their way back from the beach, the three friends were happy, **tanned**, **barefoot**, no t-shirts. Everything was great and happy in the world. Tim was driving the van slowly, the radio was on and they all enjoyed the late-afternoon sun and the drive.

They came to a large **intersection**, a big set of traffic lights where two big roads crossed. The three friends chatted happily about their great surfing day as they waited for the lights to change. The lights went green for them to turn right, and Tim **pulled off** slowly, and this is when everything changed. The crossroads was on a small hill and so cars coming the other way would come over the top of the hill and then down towards the intersection and the traffic lights. It was not really dangerous, unless someone was driving much too fast.

The van turned slowly and crossed over the lane for **oncoming** traffic. Bad timing. Another car came over the top of the hill in the opposite direction, very fast. Much too fast!

The driver of the other was driving so fast that he was quickly on them. He didn't even see the van until it was too late to **avoid** them or slow down enough. Time was driving **calmly** and did see the car that was about to hit them. Ben had his eyes closed and his arm out of the window, thinking about the big dinner they were going to get. He was hungry.

John was the only one of the three friends that saw what was about to happen. He said "oh no" very quietly to himself, and he shouted two more times as **loudly** as he could,

"**watch out** Tim.....watch out Tim!"

It was too late. The small car tried to slow down, but it hit the left corner of the van hard with a huge crashing sound of metal **crumpling** and **crushing**!

It was a big accident. Tim hit his head on the steering wheel of the van and **knocked himself out**. Ben was closest to the impact and he was very lucky because the window of the van crushed around him, but did not hurt him very much, but he did hit his hand very hard on the window of the van and almost broke it. John was really the **luckiest** of the three friends, maybe because he was the only one that saw the other car before it hit them. He was prepared, but Tim and Ben had no idea and had an even worse shock and surprise than John on impact.

John was sitting in the middle of his two friends because the front seat of the van was a bench so the three were sitting **alongside** each other. The people in a row. None of the three were wearing seat belts and so when the car hit them they were **thrown around** inside the van, which is how Tim hit his head and Ben hit his hand on the window. John was protected, between his two friends and so for him, the impact was much less.

Chapter Summary

John, Ben and Tim were driving home from their day at the beach when another person, who was driving too fast, crashed into them. There was a big impact.

Vocabulary

Tanned - to have brown skin from the sun

Barefoot - the wear nothing on your feet

Intersection - a place where two or more big roads cross each other

Pull off - to start a trip or journey

Oncoming - something coming from the opposite direction to you: approaching, advancing, nearing

Avoid - avert, bypass, dodge, escape ****

Calmly - to do something in a calm and relaxed way: serenely, sedately, smoothly ****

Loudly - to do something, or speak, in a loud way: aloud, noisily, emphatically

Watch out - to alert someone of a dangerous situation: be careful, be alert, beware

Crush - mash, squash, squeeze

Crumple - buckle, crush, crunch, collapse

Luckiest - to be the most lucky: fortuitous, fortunate, successful

Alongside - besides, next to, at the side of, close by

Thrown around - when a violent movement agitates and moves an object aggressively

Chapter Eight

Everything was confused and everybody felt like they were in a terrible dream. Tim was **knocked out** by the crash and it took him some seconds to come back to reality, with horrible pain in his head and neck. Ben was also in a bad way, the car had impacted next to where he was sitting and so he was in shock, but luckily he was not very badly hurt. Very lucky.

John was awake and aware of what had happened. The key of the van had been knocked out of the ignition of the van, so it was not possible to turn the engine off. The engine was screaming, making very loud sounds. John thought about all the films he had seen on TV and was convinced that the van engine was going to explode. He started shouting "the keys Tim, turn off the Engine, where are the keys?!"

Tim was starting to wake up, but he did not understand what had happened, and now John was shouting in his ear "the keys, the keys – quickly!" Tim did not understand anything, and couldn't find the keys.

John started looking around on the floor, but he couldn't find the keys, and he was really scared that the van was going to explode. Ben was on his left side and he started to shout at him "get out of the car, Ben you need to get out now!" Ben was also very confused, but he tried to open the door. The door did not open, it had changed shape from the impact of the accident and it was impossible to open. "Don't worry, we are ok here, let's relax here" Ben said. John realised that Ben and Tim were very confused, and he needed to get out of the Van quickly. The window was open and so he **climbed over** Ben and climbed out of the window. John had no shoes on and the road around the van was covered in broken glass, but he did not think about it and **jumped down** onto the road and broken glass. He started looking around on the floor for the keys, maybe they were outside the van on the road.

John could not find the keys on the road and he started walking around all over the broken glass trying to stop other cars to get help. Cars were still passing the accident and John realised he was confused like Ben and Tim because he walked in front of the cars, waving his arms and asking people to stop and help them. Tim was coming back to reality, and he found the keys on the floor of the van and turned off the engine. A car stopped in front of John and the driver got out to help him. John looked back and realized that the little car that had hit them was in a much worse condition. The van was big and tall, but the car was small and probably much lighter and **weaker**. The front of the small car was totally crushed and there were two people inside who were **trapped**.

The driver of the small car was really stupid! He was driving much too fast, like an idiot. But now he was trapped inside the small car with his girlfriend. It was a bad situation. John was very angry with him because the accident was his fault, but now he felt bad because they were trapped in the car. More people stopped their cars to help the three friends, and Tim and Ben slowly got out of the van. Their beautiful van was destroyed. They were not driving to Perth tomorrow, there would be no big adventure. Their amazing surf holiday with the van was finished.

Amazingly, John did not cut his feet, **even though** he was walking around over all that broken glass.

Chapter Summary

The car accident was serious, but John was not very hurt. The other car was smaller and it looked like the other people were trapped in the small car.

Vocabulary

Knocked out - when someone becomes unconscious: KO, senseless, out cold, laid out ****

Climbed over - to go over the top of somethings, using hands and feet

Jumped down - to descend, go down, by jumping

Weaker - to be less strong: feeble, fragile, frail

Trapped - to be stuck inside a place: captured, cornered

Amazingly - surprisingly, strikingly, remarkably ****

Even though - although

Chapter Nine

The ambulance arrived to start taking people to the hospital. The doctors were worried about Tim because he had **hit** his head. They wanted to take him in the ambulance to the hospital and do an X-ray on him to check if his head and neck were ok.

The driver of the car got out of his **ruined** vehicle, but his girlfriend was trapped inside. The front of the little car had collapsed and there was no space for her to get out. She said that she could not **breathe**, and it was a scary moment. At that point, a fire truck arrived and the firemen used a machine to cut the front of the car and make space for her to escape. They took the girl and the driver of the car to the hospital in one ambulance, and a second ambulance took the three friends to the same hospital.

John, Ben and Tim were still very confused and they did not have time to take their phones, or money and even shoes or clothes. They went to the hospital the same way they had left the beach, barefoot, no T-shirt or money or passports. When they arrived at the hospital, the doctors took Tim to do some tests to check if he was ok. Ben and John were ok so they went to a room to wait. They were very depressed, the trip was over, their dream holiday was finished and they did not know where the van was, or their surfboards. Nothing!

After two hours the doctors brought Tim to the same room. They said that he was ok, but he needed to stay in the hospital for a few more hours so they could check on his head, then they could leave. The police arrived at the hospital and also the father of the driver. The driver was only 18 years old, and he had passed his driving test only 10 days before the accident. He was driving much too fast, the accident was his fault and he had destroyed the three friends trip, destroyed two cars, and also almost killed his girlfriend who was trapped in the car. Luckily, the girl was ok and only had some small **cuts** and **bruises**. Everybody was lucky, but the three friends were **furious** with the driver. He had ruined everything!

Chapter Summary

Everybody went to the hospital, but everybody was ok. They were all lucky. Tim, Ben and John were very angry with the driver of the other car.

Vocabulary

Hit - impact, blow, shot, collision ****

Ruined - destroyed, demolished, smashed, wrecked

Breath - to inhale air: exhalation, inhalation, gasp, pant

Cuts - laceration, wound, gash, mark

Bruises - injury, contusion, discolouration

Furious - angry, enraged, incensed, violent

Chapter Ten

Everyone involved in the car accident was ok. The firemen helped the girl get out of the car, and now she was recovering. The driver was fine, and the three friends were not seriously injured. The surf trip was finished, the campervan was destroyed. No big adventure driving to Perth across the desert, no more beaches and holiday. The three friends planned to get some money back when they sold the campervan later, that was part of the plan and now that was impossible.

The driver of the car was responsible for all of this, and Ben, Tim and John were very angry with him and wanted him to pay for all the damages. They also wanted him to lose his **driving licence** because he was so **irresponsible**. Sadly that was not going to be possible, because the boy's father arrived at the hospital and made things really complicated for the boys.

The police were at the hospital and they started to interview the three friends, who told the police what happened and that the boy was driving very badly, stupidly, and that he was responsible for everything. The police started looking at all the information on the campervan, all the papers, insurance and other small details and discovered that there was a small travel insurance paper that was missing. When the three friends bought the campervan they forgot to register a paper and pay a small local tax. It was not a big or very important detail, and because the three boys were tourists and foreigners in Australia, the police were not very angry about this, but the boy's father decided to use this detail against the boys.

Tim was still feeling bad, with a headache, and very depressed about the accident and everything that happened. He needed the money from selling the campervan to continue his trip and now all his plans were destroyed. The driver's father found him and talked to him on his own in the hospital. Ben and John were not there to help him and Tim was confused. The father of the driver said that they did not have an insurance paper that they needed for the campervan and that this was a big problem. He was going to make a lot of trouble for them if they told the police that his son was responsible for the car accident. The man did not want his son to lose his driving licence and so he forced Tim to sign a paper saying that he was responsible for the accident. He **took advantage of** Tim!

This was very **unfair** because the idiot boy was the person responsible, but the father said that Tim could go to prison if he did not sign. Tim was tired, confused and very **stressed out** by the situation. The man told Tim that he would pay for the insurance costs if Tim signed the paper and there would be no more problems.

Tim signed the paper.

Chapter Summary

Tim was confused and agreed to sign a paper to say the accident was his fault. This was not true.

Vocabulary

Driving licence - the permission you need to drive a car

Irresponsible - lacking in good sense or behaviour: ill-considered, feckless, capricious ****

Take advantage of - to exploit a person who is weaker or less intelligent than you: exploit, trick, con, deceive ****

Unfair - a situation which lacks fairness: cruel, biased, arbitrary, discriminatory

Stressed out - anxious, frazzled, nervous, tense

Chapter Eleven

John and Ben were shocked when Tim told them that he had signed the paper to say they were **guilty** of the accident, but there was nothing they could do. At least they were not going to have more problems with the police because of the insurance paper, but it was another piece of bad news.

The doctors finished checking them and they were ready to leave the hospital, with no shoes or T-shirt and no money, they did not even have the keys for the campervan and they did not know where it was. A policeman was friendly with them and said his sister had a cheap hotel where they could stay, and they could pay after they got their money back. They could stay there tonight and tomorrow they could go look for the campervan and try to get some of their things back, he had the address of where the van had been taken. A company had collected the van and taken it to a garage for **storage**.

The policeman even gave them **a lift** to the hotel.

The three friends arrived, and the lady was nice. She gave them a small room with four beds in it, and she even had some T-shirts for them and some beach sandals they could put on their feet. She said that many guests forgot bags and clothes at the hotel and these were extra clothes and sandals and they could keep them. The boys didn't have any money for food, but they were not even hungry, they were just so tired.

Each of them had a hot shower and went to bed, there was nothing else they could do. It was late and they were so tired, but they thought it would be impossible to sleep after that very traumatic day. They got into bed and tried to relax. John closed his eyes but could not stop thinking about the accident, the accident, the accident.

Chapter Summary

The three friends are ok after the accident and go to a cheap hotel to sleep. They are very tired. The next day they will go to look for the campervan.

Vocabulary

Guilty - responsible for a mistake or crime: culpable, liable, accusable, condemned

Storage - to keep or store and object: depot, repository, stockpile

A lift - to offer to take a person to a place: a ride ****

Chapter Twelve

John opened his eyes and realised that an amazing thing had happened. John had slept, and it had been the best night of sleep in his whole life. It was amazing! He felt like he had slept for 1000 years and he was so calm. It was very early in the morning and the other two were still asleep, but John felt very fresh. John went out of the room **silently** to leave his two friends sleeping and went out of the hotel to the street. It was 7 in the morning on a Sunday and there was nobody on the street. It was completely **empty.**

That morning an amazing thing happened to John which changed his life. After the terrible accident and all the bad luck of the previous day, he was so **incredibly** happy and relaxed, happy to be alive!

John walked from the hotel into the city, but everything was totally empty. It was like one of those horror movies you see, maybe a zombie film, where somebody wakes up and the world is abandoned. John walked down the middle of the avenue, in the centre of the city, and he did not see one single person. Nobody.

The sun came up and it started to get more warm. The sky was blue and birds were singing, and John thought it was the most beautiful and fantastic day he had ever seen. He was so happy to be alive and have adventures to do. This was a very important day in John's life, maybe the most important day of his life. John decided on this day to go and do everything he had been too **scared** to do. He had so many things he wanted to do, places to visit and adventures he wanted to do, but until that day he was too scared to do them. John thought he wanted to go to visit India, and Thailand, and Africa and many other places, and on this beautiful morning, he decided he was going to do exactly that. No excuses, life is short, and he could have died in that car accident. NO MORE WAITING – DO IT NOW!

John walked around in the sun and slowly went back to the hotel. He did not see anyone on his walk, he was totally alone in the city and it was perfect. He arrived back at the hotel and Tim and Ben were now awake. They both looked terrible and Tim said he had not slept at all. He had nightmares all night about the accident and said he kept hearing John's voice shouting again and again. They did not understand why John was so relaxed and happy. He told them about his amazing walk, but they did not understand and they thought he was being very strange. Why was he so happy about their terrible disaster?

The three friends' adventure together was almost finished. They needed to go look for the campervan and try to save something from the situation, but in a few days they would go in different directions, and they would not see each other for many years.

Chapter Summary

The next day John is very happy to be alive. He has a very nice walk around the city and decides he will live his life to the full after the accident.

Vocabulary

Silently - to do something in a silent or quiet way: mutely, quietly, wordlessly, soundlessly ****

Empty - with nothing inside: barren, deserted, hollow, unfilled

Incredibly - astonishingly, amazingly, unbelievably ****

Scared - afraid, fearful, anxious, panicked, petrified

Chapter Thirteen

Later in the afternoon the three friends went to find the campervan. They had no money, but they convinced a taxi driver to take them to the address. They told him they had money there to pay him and he accepted.

When they arrived at the garage they **found out** just how destroyed their van was. It was not possible to drive anymore, their adventure was definitely over. Everything inside the van was a **mess** and it looked exactly like it had been in an accident. They found their money and passports and everything was there. The bad news was that the people from the garage said they needed to pay for the service of taking the van away from the accident. The mechanic said the van was not worth anything really. He could pay the friends $300 for the van, but the cost of taking the van from the accident was $400. It was incredible, but they had to pay the man $100 for him to keep their van. They paid him to give him their van. What a disaster!

The friends took their surfboard, backpacks, money and shoes and left the van there at the garage. Now they were 100% sure, there would be no trip to Perth, no more surf adventures. Only if they walked. They had to take the bus back to the city with all their things, they did not know where to go so they went back to the same cheap hotel. They also **owed** the lady money for the previous night. She had been very kind and **helpful**.

Tim was particularly unhappy and depressed. He was the one that was driving, he was the person who signed the paper for the other driver's father, saying he was **guilty**. He was also the person who really needed the money from selling the van to continue his holiday. For him, the trip was over and he needed to call his parents in England to send him the money to go back home. He was really sad.

As for Ben, he was from a rich family so it was not a big problem for him. He said he was going to fly to New Zealand to try to find some new travel friends. Maybe he could buy another cheap campervan in New Zealand and he could go on another surf adventure there. Maybe in New Zealand he would have better luck than in Australia!

For John, the adventure was not completely over. He had worked very hard in England before his trip and so he still had enough money to continue travelling. He had also made an important decision on that Sunday walk around the city. Now he was going to follow his dreams and do everything he had been scared of doing before the accident. His life was about to change.

Chapter Summary

The three friends find the campervan and can find their passports and money, but they lose a lot of money when they give the campervan away for free. For Tim, the holiday is finished, but for Ben and John, it will continue.

Vocabulary

Found out - to discover something new: ascertain, detect, determine, identify ****

Mess -disorder, clutter, confusion, disarray

Owed - to have to give someone money: payable, undue, overdue, in arrears ****

Helpful - a person who is kind and helps others

Guilty - responsible, culpable

Epilogue

The three needed to stay at the hotel for another few days to organize things. Tim was waiting for his flight home, Ben organizing his flight to New Zealand, and John needed to decide what to do with his life now.

Two days later John was walking around the city, thinking, when he walked past the window of a travel agent. He decided to go in and ask if they organized flights from Australia to India. The person inside explained that they had many different options, but one of the best and cheapest was a ticket which stopped first in Thailand and then continued to India. The ticket was really cheap and the person said that when John arrived in Thailand he could talk to the airline company and change the date to continue to India. He only had to pay a small amount of money to change the ticket date and he could change it three different times. It was perfect. The ticket was only one-way to India, it did not have an option to continue back to England after, but John decided it was exactly what he needed. He was still scared, but he bought the ticket and 4 days later he was going to fly to Thailand.

John walked out of the travel agents office and onto the street. He smiled and breathed the warm air. His new life was going to start, a new life of adventure. He decided that the car accident was the best thing that had ever happened to him.

The End

Final Vocabulary

Review

Story - One

In this final review section, you will find some of the most difficult, important and useful words explained and some example phrases provided. These are the words followed by **** in the vocabulary sections of each chapter.

Keen - excited, enthusiastic, eager to do something

- He was really keen to go to the beach

- I am not keen on broccoli
- The children are very keen to go to the cinema

Hang out - loiter, spend time, wait around doing nothing in particular

- Do you want to go hang out tomorrow with me?
- The kids were hanging out at the beach

Get used to - to become accustomed to, habituated to

- I am trying to get used to my new job
- People living in Russia need to get used to the cold when they are children
- It is difficult to get used to this new phone

Get to know - get to know new people or places

- I would love to get to know Paris
- I would like to get to know you better

Work out - to calculate or understand something

- We need to work out a solution to this problem
- I can't work it out!

Afford - to be able to pay for a thing, or permit yourself to do a thing

- I can't afford that Ferrari
- She can afford to go on holiday four times a year

Suddenly - When something happens quickly, in an unexpected way: abruptly, quickly, swiftly

- A man suddenly ran into the room
- It has suddenly become really hot

Scary - When a situation makes you afraid or scared, it is a scary situation:alarming, chilling, shocking

- It is really scary to be attacked by a dog!
- That film was so scary!

Whenever - Any time something happens, at any given moment

-
  I love to eat pizza whenever I go to Italy
- We can meet for a coffee whenever you like next week

Uncomfortable - not comfortable: difficult, hard, annoying

-
  The aggressive man made me feel really uncomfortable
- The argument was quite uncomfortable

Although - a modal verb to contrast: albeit, despite, even if, though

-
  I have to go out, although it is raining
- Although I love chocolate, I can't eat it every day

Break down - When a vehicle, or complicated mechanism breaks or stops working

-
- My car broke down on the way to work!
- The fax machine has broken down

Unpleasant - not nice: disagreeable, distasteful, nasty

-
  I thought that man was very unpleasant
- There is an unpleasant smell coming from the kitchen

Looking forward to - happy about something happening in the future: anticipate, count on, hope

-
  I am really looking forward to going on holiday
- The kids are looking forward to dinner

Avoid - avert, bypass, dodge, escape

- I want to avoid any bank debt
- She tries to avoid taking the bus in the morning

Calmly - to do something in a calm and relaxed way: serenely, sedately, smoothly

-
  The man spoke very calmly

Knocked out - when someone becomes unconscious: KO,

senseless, out cold, laid out

- The boxer was knocked out by his opponent

Amazingly - surprisingly, strikingly, remarkably

- NYC is an amazingly expensive city
- The film was amazingly scary

Hit - impact, blow, shot, collision

- The boxer hit his opponent and knocked him out
- The boy hit the other boy

Irresponsible - lacking in good sense or behaviour: ill-considered, feckless, capricious

- The man lost his job because he was so irresponsible

Take advantage of - to exploit a person who is weaker or less intelligent than you: exploit, trick, con, deceive

- The thieves took advantage of the old lady to steal her money

A lift - to offer to take a person to a place: a ride

- Can I give you a lift to the airport?

Silently - to do something in a silent or quiet way: mutely, quietly, wordlessly, soundlessly

- The lion approached the deer silently

Incredibly - astonishingly, amazingly, unbelievably

- The big man was incredibly strong

Found out - to discover something new: ascertain, detect, determine, identify

- When I found out how expensive the restaurant was I left
- We need to find out who the murderer is!

Owed - to have to give someone money: payable, undue, overdue, in arrears

-
  I am owed a lot of money by my friend John

- She owes me an explanation!

Did you understand all the new vocabulary and phrasal verbs in this story?

Try to practice writing phrases with this new vocabulary to help you remember it.

Remember, if you enjoyed story one and it helped you to learn more English, write a reference for this book to help other English students like you find it.

Now we will continue to story two – a tropical adventure in Brazil.

Story Two –

Carnaval in Brazil

Chapter One

Helmi is from Finland. She's from a small village in the mountains but she moved the capital to go to university and after four years Helmi has finished University but she does not really know what to do with her life now.

Helmi really loves sports and during the four years that she has been at University she has been **busily** competing in many many different sports. Hellmi has played for the University basketball team, for the netball team and for the water polo team. **However**, after many years of looking for different sports, she's finally found the thing that she most wants to do, something called Capoeira. This is a sport from Brazil which was originally created by African slaves to **be able to** **secretly** practice martial arts. Helmi is in love with capoeira. She finds it really **challenging** and great fun to do.

Now Helmi has finished University she really wants to find a new job and has been looking for several months, but it's really difficult. Helmi is volunteering at a cafe for the **homeless,** she gives them food and something to drink. In the free time that she has, Helmi practices capoeira and she's getting better and better at this.

Now Helmi needs to decide what she's going to do with her life. Part of her thinks that she should go back to her small village, stay with her parents and find something to do there. Perhaps she can work at the local supermarket, a pharmacy or some other small business. On the other hand, Helmi thinks that she should look for something outside in the world, maybe go and live **abroad**. This is something that Helmi has always wanted to do and now she finally has the opportunity to do it so she needs to decide.

Chapter Summary

Helmi has finished university and is now looking for a job and deciding what she wants to do. She has started to practice a new sport called capoeira, which originated in Brazil.

Vocabulary

Busily - to do things in a busy or quick way: hastily, hurriedly, eagerly

However - nonetheless, notwithstanding, yet ****

Be able to - the ability to do something ****

Secretly - to do things in a secret way: clandestinely, covertly, stealthily

Challenging - something difficult or hard to do

Homeless - someone with no place to live

Abroad - outside your own country

Chapter Two

Ines is from Portugal. She **grew up** in Lisbon and she has lived there all her life. After going to University and studying medicine she has now graduated and also needs to decide what she wants to do with her life. Ines lives with her parents in the north of Lisbon; she has never lived on her own.

Ines has been studying English for a long time and has been to many different language academies. Her English has improved a lot but it is still not **as good as** she wants it to be. In Portugal, it's quite difficult to find a job and in any case, salaries are quite low for newly graduated doctors like Ines. Because of this, Ines decided that it would be a great idea to go to work in London as a doctor, she has many other friends who have gone to work in Great Britain and they are **earning** really good salaries as new Junior doctors.

The main problem is that Ines still does not think that her English is good enough. She has spent the last six months studying at a Language Academy three times a week in preparation for an important English exam. This exam is called the IELTS certificate and it is very important if you want to work professionally in the United Kingdom. Ines needs to get a good score in this exam but it's very difficult, her English is quite good, but not good enough for the result that she needs. Ines spends every weekend studying extra time, watching TV series in English, reading books, and all types of other studies to try and improve her English and pass this exam.

Finally, in March, Ines is ready to do the exam. She needs a 7.5 in the exam and she is nervous in the morning as she drives to the examination centre. Ines does quite well in the exam, but **unfortunately**, she is still really nervous and this affects her final result. When the results finally come, Ines is really disappointed, she tried as hard as possible and she really has improved her English a lot in the last few months, but she only got a 6.5 in the exam, she is really **upset** and does not know what to do. The next available exam date is four months in the future and now she needs to decide what she wants to do, should she try to study even more and try to do the exam again, or should she try to do something else and continue to study English in a more relaxed way? The exam costs a lot of money to do and she **borrowed** the money from her father to do the exam the first time. She feels bad about this and she does not want to ask her father for more money unless she is 100% sure that she will pass the next exam.

Chapter Summary

Ines has graduated from medical school and is thinking about going to live in London to work. Ines tried to pass the IELTS English exam, but she did not get the result she wanted.

Vocabulary

Grow up - to get older in a place ****

As good as - to be equally positive to another thing ****

Earning - the money you are making: acquire, collect, gain

Unfortunately - sadly, regrettably, lamentably

Upset - to be unhappy or discontent about something: agitated, disconcerted, aggrieved

Borrow - to ask for a thing or money from another person: rent, obtain, mooch

Chapter Three

Helmi continues to practice capoeira and she continues to get better. That Summer she represents her capoeira Club in the national championships and does really well, she comes second, which is a really fantastic result considering she has only been training for 6 months. Helmi's capoeira instructor can see that she has lots of potential and he wants to **encourage** her to train more and to **get better**.

After this fantastic result, Helmi **redoubles** her efforts to try and improve and this is great because she really does not have anything else to do at this time. Helmi gets a job working in a cafe, but it isn't really something that she wants to do with her life or particularly interesting and after a couple of weeks she **quits**. She prefers to concentrate more on this new sport that she is growing to love more and more every day.

As an **unemployed** person, Helmi can get quite a lot of help from the government because Finland has a very generous **social security** system. Helmi gets enough money per month that she does not really need to **worry** about her **bills**, but Finland is quite an expensive country so she definitely is not rich. Helmi begins to think that maybe if she went to another country, a cheaper country, this amount of money, which is not very much in Finland, could actually make her rich somewhere else!

Helmi's capoeira instructor eventually invites her to go to Brazil to train. He says to her,

"why don't you go? you can really be good at this sport and I know you don't really have anything else to do, I have a friend in Brazil who would be very happy to receive you and you can train at his Club. I think this would be a really good adventure for you and very interesting. You should give it a try."

Helmi does not really need to think about it for a very long time, after only a couple of days she calls her instructor and tells him that she thinks it's a great idea. She's going to go to Brazil to practise capoeira for a few months, this is going to be a great adventure for her. Helmi is excited about her trip and really **looking forward to** getting to know a new and exciting foreign country. Helmi has never lived abroad, and apart from a few short trips around Europe, she has never really travelled anywhere exotic or far away before. This is going to be a great adventure and she can really **get into** this new sport that she loves so much. Brazilian Capoeira.

Chapter Summary

Helmi is invited to visit Brazil to train capoeira and decides this will be a good idea. She will go to Brazil for several months.

Vocabulary

Encourage - boost, buoy, embolden, inspire ****

Get better - to improve at a thing: develop, enhance, progress ****

Redouble - to make two times the effort: enhance, magnify, strengthen

Quit - to stop or give up something: depart, drop out, retire, renounce

Unemployed - to have no job: inactive, jobless, between jobs

Social security - a system to give homeless people help and money

Worry - to be concerned: concern, anguish, fear, misery

Bills - electricity and gas costs

Look forward to - to be excited about a thing in the future: anticipate, hope, anxious for ****

Get into - Become more addicted to a thing ****

Chapter Four

Ines has also been trying to get a job for several months. After failing her exam she decided that it would be a good idea to try to get some work experience so that she had more time to study for the next exam. **Therefore**, Ines began to work as a medical assistant at a private hospital. This was not the dream job that she really wanted, she would not be able to work as a full-time doctor, but for now, it was better than nothing and at least it helped her to **save up** some money.

Ines continues with this job for several months, but, just like Helmi, she decides that this is really not for her and begins to feel a little bit **anxious** to do something new with her life. Ines knows that she is still not ready to do the IELTS exam again, but does not really have any other ideas. She is going to **keep on** working, and trying to improve her English in her **spare time**.

It was no Christmas time and, like so many families in Portugal, Ines went to visit her grandparent's village in the mountains. There were family members from all different parts of Portugal, many cousins and aunts and uncles that Ines had not seen for a long time. Ines, like many families in Portugal, has family living abroad. There are Portuguese communities in the United States, many people living in

France and Belgium, and of course, there are connections with Portugal's Old Colonial countries such as Brazil. Ines actually has quite a lot of family in Brazil, because her uncle went there in the 1970s to work, and never came back. He married a woman there and so Ines has many cousins living in Brazil that she has never visited, even though many members of her Brazilian family had come to Portugal for weddings and other family occasions. Ines really likes the Brazilian side of her family and one cousin, in particular, called Gloria, who lives in Rio de Janeiro.

Ines' cousin Gloria is visiting Portugal for Christmas, she is on her summer holidays because the winter in Europe is the summertime in Brazil and December is one of the hottest months of the year. Gloria talks to Ines about her frustrations in Portugal with work and her life and decides to invite Ines to go and stay with her in Brazil. Just like Helmi, back in Finland, Ines really did not need to think about this for too long, she had always wanted to go to Brazil, and she really likes her Brazilian cousins who she has gotten to know during the different times they have visited Portugal. Ines decided this would be a great opportunity to think about her life and to take time studying, she could always take her English books with her and spend time studying every day while she was on holiday. She told her cousin the same evening,

"yes, of course, I will go with you to Brazil, this is going to be fantastic fun!"

Chapter Summary

At Christmas time, Ines is invited to go to Brazil by her cousin Gloria. Ines decides to go to Brazil.

Vocabulary

Therefore - As a consequence of which: accordingly, so, then ****

Save up - to accumulate money for a future plan

Anxious - concerned, distressed, nervous

Keep on - to continue with: last, insist ****

Spare time - the extra time you have, free time

Chapter Five

Rio de Janeiro is one of the most amazing cities in the world, it is commonly known as 'The Marvelous City'. People from all over the world go to Rio de Janeiro for its famous beaches, its Carnival and Street parties. Even in Brazil, Rio de Janeiro is a famous place, and lots of Brazilians from other places go there on holiday. So many people dream of Rio and, for Helmi, the day she arrived in Rio de Janeiro was amazing, the weather was hot, the sky was blue, and there were new and exotic smells and sights on every street corner.

Helmi rented a small place in Copacabana where she could stay that was not far from the place she was going to train Capoeira. There are many apartments in Brazil that used to have a small **Maid's** apartment at the back of the house. Sometimes, these places even have a separate entrance and a separate elevator so that the maid could enter into the back of the house without the family knowing. **Nowadays**, many families in Brazil do not pay for a maid to live with them and so these small rooms, complete with a small toilet and shower, are **often** left empty, and now families **tend to** put things that they don't need there. These rooms sometimes just **turn into junk** rooms.

However, some people now rent out these small spaces for tourists. In fact, these are perfect spaces to rent if you're on holiday in Brazil because they are like a small, mini-apartment, they have access to the kitchen, a small toilet, a small living room and, with the separate elevator entrance, these small spaces feel like your own private apartment. Helmi found this place available in Copacabana online, there were three students who lived there and they made some extra money by renting out this **empty** maid's room that they did not use. For Helmi this was going to be perfect, it even had a small washing machine so she could wash her clothes.

After **settling into** this new place, Helmi spent the next several days exploring this amazing city and she began to fall in love immediately. The views were incredible, the beaches were amazing, with beautiful **tanned** people running up and down the sand all day long. It seemed like nobody needed to go to work and nobody was in a **rush** to go **anywhere**, it seems like the city where everyone was on holiday all the time. It was wonderful. Helmi realised why this city was so famous around the world and why it was considered one of the best and most interesting places for tourists to visit anywhere. It really was true, this was an amazing place, it was so different from Finland, so warm and hot and people seemed to be so happy. Helmi felt content that she had made a great decision and that being in Rio de Janeiro was so much better than being back in Finland, in the rain and the snow and the cold, looking for a job and not knowing what to do with her life.

Chapter Summary

Helmi arrives in Rio de Janeiro and starts to explore the city. She rents a small place to stay. She really likes the city.

Vocabulary

Maid - a person who helps you clean your house

Nowadays - today, current, up to date ****

Often - frequently, repeatedly, usually, many times ****

Tend to - the tendency to do something ****

Turn into - to become something ****

Junk - clutter, debris, rubbish, trash

However - a contrasting modal verb ****

Empty - with nothing inside: bare, barren, deserted

Settle into - to become more comfortable, ready to live in a place

Tan - to be brown from the sun

Rush - to be in a hurry, or late, for something ****

Anywhere - any possible place

Chapter Six

Ines arrives in Brazil only a short time after Helmi. Her cousins **pick her up** from the airport and take her to their house. Just like Helmi, Ines falls in love with Brazil really quickly, and for all the same reasons. It is all so different from back in Portugal where people are much more serious and perhaps don't know how to live life **to the full**, not like these Brazilians.

However, the main difference between the two girls is that Ines can speak the language, even though perhaps many Brazilians don't understand her accent very well. There is actually a big difference between the Portuguese that is spoken in Brazil and in Portugal, and even though many Portuguese people can understand Brazilians very well, because there is so much Brazilian TV that they grow up watching, in Brazil it is a different story. Brazilian sometimes have a real problem understanding Portuguese people because it is an accent that they are not used to. In addition to this, Portuguese people conjugate many verbs in a different way from the way that they are used to speaking in Brazil, so many Brazilians, hearing a person from Portugal speak for the first time, can get quite confused, even though it is the same language.

Ines finds this out in the first week in Brazil. Her cousins understand her perfectly well, but when they go out to restaurants, and when Ines goes out to explore on her own and stops for a coffee or something to eat, she finds out that a lot of people have difficulty understanding her, which **becomes** very frustrating!

"This is ridiculous," Ines thinks,

"I am speaking the same language and they do not even understand me!"

Ines quickly realizes that she needs to change her accent a little bit for people to understand her, she tries to pronounce some words a little more like the way Brazilians speak and to reduce her strong Lisbon accent. This starts to work, and people begin to understand her, even though a lot of them have a confused look on their face, and others often make jokes about her funny accent.

Nevertheless, Ines' first week in Brazil is a fantastic adventure as she gets used to the hot weather, the different food and different people. Her cousins in Brazil are really welcoming to her and they are so happy that she has come to visit and Ines decides there is no real reason to go back to Europe in a **hurry**. She feels like maybe she never wants to go back!

The only problem on this fantastic holiday is that Ines does not find any time to study English, she is having enough difficulty just trying to learn the different dialects of Portuguese, she does not have time for any English study. The original idea was that she would be able to find at least a couple of hours each day to study English, however, this is proving to not be the case **at all**. Ines is far too **busy** enjoying life, learning how to dance Samba, going to the beach every day and generally having the best time in her life. She is not thinking about English or the stupid IELTS exam anymore, just about having fun in Rio de Janeiro, this marvellous City!

Chapter Summary

Ines loves Brazil and is having a very good time. Some people do not understand her accent when she speaks Portuguese. She does not have time to study English.

Vocabulary

Pick up - to collect a person or thing

To the full - to the maximum, make the most of

Become - turn into

Nevertheless - similar to regardless of, despite which ****

Hurry - rush

At all - not in any way ****

Busy - to be occupied: active, hustling, persevering

Chapter Seven

There was going to be a big party to celebrate **Ines' cousin's** birthday and a big group of friends were going to go out to an area of the city called Lapa. This is a historic, Colonial, area in the centre of Rio De Janeiro, which nowadays can be found full of bars and people dancing and celebrating. Samba comes out of the window of **sweaty,** hot, small and **dark** bars where hundreds of people can be seen dancing inside. People sell food and drinks on the street. Especially that national drink caipirinha, and people **stroll** around and enjoy the music, the sights and the people. It is the first time that Ines has visited this area, Lapa, and she is surprised and amazed by how exotic everything seems to be, lots of the old buildings look to be almost **falling down**. It all seems so different from Portugal and she loves it.

It is the first time that Gloria's friends have met someone from Portugal and they all have a great time **finding out** about her life in Lisbon, and laughing a little at her accent. They are all going to a party later in the evening, but first, they are meeting for some drinks and some street food. There are lots of shows in the street, **buskers**, street musicians, and people selling all sorts of different things. There is an amazingly **wide variety** of street food, lots of things that Ines has never seen before in her life.

Ines has fun following the group around and they stop to look at a street show. It is a capoeira show, and this is the first time that it never has seen this amazing Brazilian art form which she has heard off before. This style of dancing, or martial arts, was brought to Brazil by African slaves and then developed, in secret, on sugar plantations in the Northeast of Brazil. It needed to be developed in secret because the Portuguese wanted to defend against any type of organization or militarisation by the African slaves, so they developed capoeira and **pretended** that it was a dance. In reality, it was a way for them to practice martial arts and to develop a way to defend themselves in secret.

Ines watched the capoeira show in fascination and was amazed by the black bodies jumping and spinning around each other, sweaty in the hot tropical night. But, there was one person in this big group of dancers who **stood out**, a small blond girl with bright blue eyes, she did not look like any of the other Brazilians there, in fact, she really did not look Brazilian at all.

Chapter Summary

Ines goes to an area of the city called Lapa. This is a place with many parties and bars. Ines sees Helmi performing capoeira in the street.

Vocabulary

Ines's cousin's - the possessive can multiply *****

Sweaty - to sweat a lot

Dark - no light: dim, dingy, drab

Stroll - a relaxed walk

Fall down - fall to the floor ****

Find out - to discover new information: ascertain, detect, determine

Buskers - people playing music for money on the street

Wide variety - a lot of different options

Pretend - impersonate, feign, fool, affect

Stand out - attract attention, be distinct, highlighted, striking

Chapter Eight

This is when Ines met Helmi. After the capoeira show, she introduced herself and said the show was amazing and she really wanted to learn how to do it, but Helmi looked at her in confusion and Ines realized that this girl did not actually speak Portuguese. This was great, it was a chance to practice her English, which she had started to forget now that she was in Brazil. The two girls realised that even though they were from two very different countries they had many things in common, and they spent the rest of the evening having a great time together in Lapa, going to lots of different samba parties with Ines' cousin and her friends. At the end of the night, the girls made plans to meet the next day to see some of the city together.

The girls met the next day in the afternoon at a famous place in

Ipanema which is called Arpoador. In English this means 'the harpooner', a person who uses a **harpoon,** probably to hunt whales or some other large animal in the sea. This is a famous place between the two beaches of Copacabana and Ipanema where many people go to see the **sunset**, you can see all of the favelas and the beautiful mountains of Rio De Janeiro in the background, behind Ipanema, and the sunset there is fantastic. The girls talked about how much they were both beginning to fall in love with Brazil and how they really wanted to experience more of this amazing country, and later that evening they went out together around the city to eat at a nice restaurant where they tried some new food. The food was very different from what they had already tried and they later found out this food was from the northeast of Brazil. They thought it was wonderful and started talking about how other places in Brazil could be so different from Rio de Janeiro because the country was so big and varied.

"Why don't we go together to the North-East of Brazil for Carnival?" Ines said to her new friend.

"I realize that I have only known you for one day but we both want to see Brazil and we both want an adventure. Let's just go and try!"

Helmi was really enjoying her capoeira classes in Rio de Janeiro but she knew that Carnival was **coming up** soon and she had already started to think about what she might do to enjoy this festival so she thought to herself that it would be a great idea to go somewhere else for one or two weeks and then she could always come back to you and continue after that. It would be a holiday inside a holiday.

They didn't know anything about the North-East of Brazil, they didn't have any friends there, they didn't know how much the tickets would cost, they didn't even know if it was possible to go up there last minute, but they decided to give it a try. Carnival was only two weeks away so maybe everything was already **booked**. Ines told Helmi that she would ask her cousins and see what they said they made a plan to meet the next day and see if they could organize everything. A new adventure was going to start again and they were both excited.

Chapter Summary

Ines and Helmi decide to go to a different place in Brazil to celebrate carnaval, a party which happens every year after Easter.

Vocabulary

Harpoon - something used to fish or hunt for big animals

Sunset - when the sun goes down

Coming up - something approaching in the future ****

Booked - to reserve something: contracted, engaged, reserved, lined up

Chapter Nine

That same night Ines went back to her cousin's house and asked them what they thought about her plan to go up to the Northeast, and **luckily** one of Vanessa's cousin's not only thought it was a great idea but also had a contact for her.

"'I have a really good friend from University who lives in a beautiful place called Olinda, this is a small Colonial city which is really close to his Recife, in the Northeast, in a state called Pernambuco." Ines' cousin said.

"I have been there many times and it's a really fantastic place, I love it, and Carnival there is really special. I will call my friend, but I am sure that she would be happy to let you stay. You should definitely go, it's a great idea!"

So, that was that - it was decided. The next day Ines told Helmi great news. They had a look online the same day and found tickets which were not too expensive. They bought the tickets, and now they had a place to stay and a recommendation from her cousin so it was going to be much easier than they thought. They booked one-way tickets because they did not know what would happen with the adventure and Ines' cousin's friend had told them that they could stay for as long as they wanted. Fantastic!

The new friends spent the next couple of weeks seeing each other sometimes in Rio to visit tourist places, and Helmi made the most of the time to practice capoeira every day before the trip to the North-East. They went to some amazing places in Rio de Janeiro such as the 'Christ Redeemer' statue which is a huge, and famous, statue that can be found on a mountain with a view of the whole city. Another amazing tourist place that they visited was a place called the Sugarloaf, in Portuguese, it is called the 'pao de açuca'. This is a famous hill in the Centre of Rio which has incredible sunsets over the city, and you need to take the **funicular** to go up to the top. Although it is a little bit expensive, it is definitely **worthwhile**. What an amazing place!

The two weeks **went by** really quickly and, before the girls even knew what happened, the day when they were to fly to the northeast of Brazil was already here, they met in the morning in Copacabana together and took a taxi to the airport. The flight was short and **uneventful** and, very quickly, they found themselves in Recife, a totally different place from Rio de Janeiro. They took another taxi to the small city of Olinda which was about 15 or 20 minutes away, on the other side of the big beautiful bay. The girls arrived only two or three days before Carnival was ready to start and they could see it was going to be a **huge** party.

Chapter Summary

The two friends visit some beautiful tourist sites in Rio, and then go to the city of Olinda, in the North-East. Carnaval is about to start.

Vocabulary

Luckily - in a fortunate way: opportunely, fortuitously, favourably

Funicular - a hanging cabin, on cables: cable car

Worthwhile - something which is good or worth the effort: beneficial, worthy, rewarding

Went by - time that passes *goes by* ****

Uneventful - nothing much happens: boring, tedious, unexciting ****

Huge - very big: giant, colossal, great, immense

Chapter Ten

when they arrived in the small town of Olinda they could see that it was going to be something special because the house where they were going to stay was amazing. It was a beautiful Old Colonial House, in fact, almost all the houses in the centre of Olinda were beautiful old colonial houses painted in so many different colours. This house was painted all in blue and it had a huge garden behind it with a swimming pool and another small house behind the swimming pool. It was a beautiful old space full of **charm**, but the most beautiful thing about the house was that there was a very large mango tree in the middle of the back garden. It was mango season, and it seemed like it was too good to be true, but up to a dozen or more mangoes would fall from the tree every day and you could **pick them up** in the morning and open them with your hands and eat them for breakfast. Helmi thought this was the most amazing thing she had ever seen, in Finland it is cold and there are no tropical fruits, if you want to buy a mango in a supermarket in Finland it will be very very expensive, and here you could wake up in the morning pick one up off the floor and eat it for breakfast with your hands, with the juice running down your arms and all over your hands. Then, you could just jump into the swimming pool surrounded by all the other nature in the garden, Helmi really thought she was in Paradise.

It was a big house with four or five bedrooms and several friends lived there together, they were university students in the city of Recife and they took the bus across the bay every day. Everybody in the house had a lot of friends who were visiting for carnaval, and the girls quickly realised that this was also something of a business in this town. Because this was such a popular place for tourists from around Brazil, and around the world, to go to the carnival, many people rented bedrooms and even sofas or a piece of floor for carnaval. The town was going to be absolutely **packed**. In this case, Gloria's friend, the owner of the house, explained to them that this was how they paid for a lot of things they needed to do in the house because everyone who stayed for carnaval was going to give them some money and, altogether, this was going to pay for renovations to the house and other things that they needed to do. They were also going to pay for two ladies to come and prepare breakfast and lunch for all the visitors every day, as well as a man to come and clean the pool every day, and even a person who was going to stand on the front door and check who was coming into the house. There were going to be so many people in Olinda for carnaval, the place was going to be so packed, that they needed to control the access to the house like it was some kind of night club.

Wow, this party is really going to be crazy, they thought to themselves. How exciting!

Chapter Summary

The house in the small city of Olinda is amazing and old. Olinda is going to be very full for carnaval. There is going to be a big party.

Vocabulary

Charm - appeal, charisma, grace, attractiveness

Pick up - to collect a person or thing from a place ****

Packed - to be very full: crowded, filled, loaded, overflowing

Chapter Eleven

And that was exactly how it was, the carnival in Olinda was absolutely incredible and the streets of the small town were packed with people, it looked like millions of people in the small town. At times it was like a football game or a big demonstration, there were so many people that Helmi and Ines felt like their feet did not touch the ground. In fact, on the first day of Carnaval, Helmi made the mistake of going out of the front door of the house in the middle of the day and there were so many people moving around that she was **swept away** with this **tide** and it was impossible to go back in the other direction, pushing against hundreds of people all moving and shouting and singing, it was incredible. Helmi had to go all the way around the block of houses and the road behind the house to come back in the same direction, making a big circle around the town. It took her almost 2 hours to get back to the same place and when she arrived back Ines was waiting for her.

"Where did you go!?" Ines shouted at her, "you disappeared!"

"This party really is crazy." Helmi Said. "I have never seen anything like this!"

Not only was the town completely packed, but the blue house was also completely packed inside. Each person who lived in the house had invited several different friends to come and there must have been more than 20 people in the house, there were people everywhere, on the floor, sleeping on the sofa, in all the beds and any other available space. The girls felt bad because the owner of the house had not asked them for any money, and they knew that the other people were contributing, but she said that she did not expect them to give her anything. **Even so**, the girls spoke to each other and decided it would be a good thing to make a small donation for all of the effort and the costs that the people were making, so they decided that at the end of Carnival they would put some money in an envelope and give it to the house owner to say thank you.

In the **meantime**, they continued to have a great time, and one thing they realised was just how much Brazilians seemed to love Carnival, people were so excited to be there and this was the highlight of their year. They saved up a lot of money to go to Carnival, they took time off work, and this was the time of the year for them to enjoy themselves and to really go crazy. That is what made this party so special, and it was like nothing that the two girls had ever seen before. There is nothing like this in Portugal and definitely nothing like this in Finland, it was really different from anything they had experienced before.

Chapter Summary

The small city of Olinda is full of people and the house is also full of people. Ines and Helmi decide to contribute with some money.

Vocabulary

Swept away - we sweep with a brush, and to be swept away means to be moved quickly by a powerful force ****

Tide - the movement of the oceans

Even so - still, though, although, yet, but ****

Meantime - something happening at the same time as another thing: interim, meanwhile, concurrently

Chapter Twelve

On the second day of Carnaval, the girls were already **exhausted**, but somebody came to wake them up very very early in the morning. A new street party was going to happen before the sun came up and it was one of the most famous street parties of the whole Carnival. It was really only for local people, and that was why it was so early in the morning, while the tourists were still sleeping and suffering from **hangovers** from the night before. But the locals we're getting up early to go to this secret street party.

Everyone in the house was going and they insisted the two girls went with them, even though nobody in the house, including Ines or Helmi, had slept more than two or three hours because the party the night before had seemed to go on forever. The two girls were really tired, but they decided that they should go, this was why they had gone to the Northeast for Carnival, for new experiences. More than 20 people from the house went out onto the street and walked down several small streets to find where the party was, it was before 7 in the morning and the sun was only just coming up. It really was **worthwhile**, there was a band who were playing carnival music and hundreds of people following them through the streets shouting and singing, even though it was really early, and most of the people there had **hardly** slept, everyone was so happy to be there.

This type of carnival party in Brazil is cold up 'bloco', this is a type parade which is typical in carnaval as the band plays music and travels along the street, they are followed by lots of people, dancing and singing with them This bloco, on the second day of Carnival, was one of the most traditional in Olinda and the girls had a great time, but as it got later and more and more people joined it, the bloco started to get a little out of control. There were so many people following the band, and the crowds grew and grew as more people woke up and came to the party, that things started to feel a little dangerous. In the middle of all of these people, there was a **rope**, a long rope, which went around the band, volunteers holding it. The idea of this rope was to stop the crowd from **crushing** the band.

A person who the girls had met in the house started shouting at them that they should all try to get into the middle of the party, to try to **reach** the rope. The girls thought this was totally crazy but, **carried away** by the moment, they agreed, and into the middle of the crowd, they pushed and pushed until they made it to the rope. They **grabbed** it and held on **tightly**.

Chapter Summary

A street party starts very early in the morning. More and more people join the party and the girls are convinced to push into the middle of all the people.

Vocabulary

Exhausted - to be very tired: drained, bush, beat, spent

Hangovers - to feel bad the day after drinking too much alcohol

Worthwhile - for something to have been worth the effort or money: beneficial, excellent, justifiable ****

Hardly - almost not at all: barely, almost not, rarely, seldom ****

Bend - turn, twist, curve, angle, corner, curvature

Rope - a material used to tie or bind things: cord, string, cable, strand, twine

Crushing - a very strong force pressing onto an object: push, press, mash ****

Reach - to extend or arrive at a place

Carried Away - to get excited, lose control: bewitched, captivated, intoxicated, possessed ****

Grabbed - to take hold of something strongly: capture, clutch, grip, grasp, seize

Tightly - very tight, not loose: firmly, solidly, securely, hard

Chapter Thirteen

The crowd **surged**, pushed and crushed against the band, which pushed and **shoved** back at the crowd. Helmi and Ines could feel the pressure from all the people behind them, pushing against them and they started to feel more and more scared. As the huge crowd moved along the avenue it reached a **narrower** place in the road, there were cars parked on either side and people started to climb over the cars. Suddenly, Helmi almost **fell** to the ground and went under the crowd, but Ines managed to grab her arm and hold her up - this situation was getting really bad!

The band and the crowd were now moving towards a corner in the road, where things were going to get very **tight**. All of these people would have to go around this tight corner to the left and the two girls did not know how it was going to be possible for so many to **fit into** such a small place. Everybody was still dancing and pushing, jumping and shouting. They were all having a great time and did not seem to think any of this was dangerous. But it was.

"We should get out of here as soon as possible!" Hemi shouted.

The girls had to make a huge effort to escape from the middle of the huge crowd of people, they were trying to get out when everyone else was still trying to push into the centre. They pushed and shoved and shouted, and they finally managed to get out of the main part of the crown and away from the band, **sweating** and **breathing heavily**. Ines had lost one of her sandals and Helmi had lost her sunglasses too. What a **crush**!

Chapter Summary

The middle of the party was dangerous because so many people were pushing. Helmi and Ines needed to escape.

Vocabulary

Surged - a big force pushing at once: flow, swell, rise, outpouring

****

Shove - push, grab, drive, force, propel, thrust

Narrower - to be narrow if the opposite of wide: limited, constricted

****

Fell - to fall in the past tense: collapse, go down, plummet, slump

Fit into - to enter into a space ****

Sweating - to perspire from physical activity or heat: perspire, drip, ooze, secrete, seep

Breathing heavily - to breath in an intense way from exertion or strong physical activity ****

Crush - a strong pressing force: squash, squeeze, mash, push, press

Chapter Fourteen

The two girls **managed to** get out of the crush on the crowd and made it back to the house, where they had a shower, ate some food and took the chance to relax a little **while** all the other people were still out of the house at different parties. This Carnival was definitely an amazing experience, but it was a bit too much for them and they decided that it would be a good moment to try to **get out of** Olinda and go somewhere a little more relaxed. They spent the rest of the afternoon relaxing at the house and even **managed to** sleep a little bit. Afterwards, the rest of the people came back, **exhausted**, **dirty**, and **sunburnt** from the party and they talked to the house owner.

"We really love being here in your house, but I think we will go somewhere to relax for a few days," Ines told her,

"Do you think you could help us try to find a car to rent if that is possible?"

The house owner thought they were crazy to miss Carnival, this was the best time of the year, 'how strange tourists can be' she thought to herself, but okay she could help them find a car to rent, **although** it was going to be a little difficult in the middle of Carnaval. Everything was so busy and packed.

Luckily, the owner of the house knew a person, who knew a person, who could rent them a car and so the next morning the girls, carrying all of the heavy bags and pushing through the crowds and the parties, went to the outskirts of Olinda, where they picked up a car. They paid the guy for one week of rental and set off to the north of the city, along the tropical coast. First, they would drive to a city called Joao Pessoa, which was two or three hours to the north, but along the way, there were some beautiful places to visit, including an old Dutch fort which had been there since the 15th century. They stopped there for the afternoon to have some lunch, happy to be away from the crowds and all the **madness** of Carnival. **Afterwards**, they continued to the city, where they found a nice quiet hotel for a good price.

Ines and Helmi spent the next couple of afternoons on the beach, relaxing in the sun, swimming in the sea, eating crabs with beer, and generally having a great time. Much more relaxed, there were hardly any other people there.

Chapter Summary

The two girls rent a car and leave carnaval. They go to a small city called Joao Pessoa, to relax a little.

Vocabulary

Manage to - to be able to, achieve, to do something ****

While - at the same time: whilst, simultaneously, concurrently ****

Get out of - to leave, escape ***

Exhausted - to be very tired: drained, fatigued, sleepy

Dirty - not clean: filthy, messy, stained

Sunburnt - to have your skin burnt by the hot sun

Although - comparative: even though, albeit, despite ****

Madness - a crazy or mad situation: craziness, lunacy, silliness

Afterwards - after a previous thing ****

Chapter Fifteen

The city of Joao Pessoa was generally really pleasant and had some old Portuguese colonial places to visit, one of which was a fort that the Portuguese established when they had first arrived in the areas, centuries before. Joao Pessoa was one of the first places the Portuguese had colonized in Brazil, and they had set up a small fortification to protect themselves as they established the colony in the area. The two girls visited this place the next day and it was really cool, there were old castle walls with cannons, and old beautiful blue and white Portuguese style tiles on the inside of some of the rooms. It really felt like a historical place and reminded Ines of places she knew in Lisbon.

The girls were very happy to have their rental car, which gave them much more freedom to do **whatever** they wanted, and even though they thought about maybe going back down to carnaval again, in the end, they decided they were having a much better time being relaxed here than if they went back to all of that **craziness** in Olinda! So, they just decided to enjoy their time, went to different beaches, walked around the city, and generally had fun meeting new people, experiencing new foods and generally enjoying the warm tropical Sun

Neither of the two girls really had any plans for the immediate future, apart from having the car for another four or five days, they didn't really have any other responsibilities or things that they had to do. **Neither** of them even had a return ticket to Rio or to some other place in Brazil because they thought they would organize it after Carnival, and even though Helmi had promised she would go back down to Rio De Janeiro to continue her capoeira training, there was not really a big rush to do so. They were free to do **whatever** they wanted and go **wherever** they wanted, money permitting of course.

"Why don't we just call the guy and ask to rent this car for a month?" Helmi said.

"It really isn't very expensive, and to be honest, the money I get from my **unemployment benefit** back in Finland, is more than enough to pay for this, it really isn't a problem at all."

"Why don't we just continue, we can drive up to the north of Brazil, visit new places, we can just choose **random** places on the map and stop there, we can really do anything we want, at least for the next month, and then we can bring the car back, it isn't a problem." she continued.

Ines had the same feeling as when she was back in Portugal at that family Christmas dinner, and once again, she really did not need to think about this proposal for very long. She knew it was a great idea, and it was what she really wanted to do, so of course, she said yes

Chapter Summary

Ines and Helmi are much happier now and decide not to go back to carnaval. They decide to rent the car for more time and continue their trip together.

Vocabulary

Whatever - Anything that happens: any, everything, whatsoever ****

Craziness - a crazy or bizarre situation: madness, lunacy, silliness

Neither - not one or the other ****

Wherever - in any possible place ****

Unemployment Benefit - money you receive from the government when not working

Random - not selected: arbitrary, irregular, unplanned

Epilogue

The city of Fortaleza is another five hundred kilometres to the north on the coast of Brazil, Ines and Helmi have now passed that City, and they have just kept on going. Maybe they will need to turn around soon and take the car back down to Olinda, or maybe they will call the guy and extend the rental again. He was happy for the money and happy to rent it for as long as they wanted and even gave them a big discount. so perhaps they will just keep on going, who knows.

Helmi is even talking about driving the car all the way up to the Amazon, paying somebody to drive it back down to Olinda for them, and then taking a boat across the Amazon to Peru. At first, Ines thought she was crazy, but after a few days, she realised that she was serious about it, and now the idea is starting to turn from a joke into something more serious

 "You know we can take a boat in the City of Belem" Helmi keeps saying,

"That boat goes up the Amazon River for 10 days until it reaches the city of Manaus, and there we can take a second boat which will go all across the rest of the Amazon until it reaches Peru, did you know that was possible, it's amazing isn't it?!"

Who knows, maybe Helmi will even manage to convince Ines to go with her, and who knows what they will find in Peru. In any case, Ines feels a long way now from when she was back in Lisbon, working at a job she didn't like and wondering what she would do with her life.

For now, their adventure continues, and nobody knows where it's going to end, not even them. One thing we can say for sure is that they are both happy and content and looking forward to whatever comes next.

Final

vocabulary

review

However - nonetheless, notwithstanding, yet

-
  I love pizza. However, my wife hates it
- Paris is a great city with good food. However, it can be very expensive

Be able to - the ability to do something

-
  Sorry, I was not able to do my homework!
- Do you think you will be able to come to the party?

Grow up - to get older in a place

-
  I grew up in England
- She is growing up so fast

As good as - to be equally positive to another thing

-
  She is not as tall as her brother
- Try to do it as well as possible
- He is just as good at football as his little brother

Encourage - boost, buoy, embolden, inspire

-
  I hope this book encourages you to study more English
- My mother has always encouraged me to do my best

Get better - to improve at a thing: develop, enhance, progress

-
  Your English is getting better and better!
- I hope to get better at tennis

Look forward to - to be excited about a thing in the future: anticipate, hope, anxious for

-
  I am really looking forward to my summer holidays

Get into - Become more addicted to a thing

-
  I have really gotten into this new TV series
- I am getting into my new book

Therefore - As a consequence of which: accordingly, so, then

-
  You are studying English. Therefore, you will improve!

Keep on - to continue with: last, insist

- You should keep on studying

Nowadays - today, current, up to date

- Nowadays, English is more important than ever

Often - frequently, repeatedly, usually, many times

- I often play football with my friends
- I have often thought about visiting Australia

Tend to - the tendency to do something

- I tend to visit my mother on Sundays
- She tends to shout a lot

Turn into - to become something

- My small puppy has turned into a big dog!
- He turns into an idiot when he is drunk!

However - a contrasting modal verb

-

I would love to speak Chinese. However, it is very difficult to learn

- It is often cold in Russia. However, today it was hot

Rush - to be in a hurry, or late, for something

-
  I am in a big rush to get to work
- It is rush hour, there is a lot of traffic

Nevertheless - similar to despite of which

-
  I love London because it is so dynamic and busy. Nevertheless, the weather is terrible!

At all - not in any way

-
  I do not like tomatoes at all

Ines's cousin's - the possessive can multiply

-
  That is John's brother's friend's car
- I love my father's friend's dog

Fall down - fall to the floor

- The building fell down in the earthquake
- The man fell down when he was drunk

Coming up - something approaching in the future

- The party is coming up next week

Went by - time that passes *goes by*

- Time goes by fast when you are having fun
- The holiday went by too fast and now I am at work again

Uneventful - nothing much happens: boring, tedious, unexciting

- The flight was uneventful and I slept the whole way
- The film was boring and uneventful

Pick up - to collect a person or thing from a place

- Can you pick me up from the airport tomorrow?
- I need to pick up a package for my friend

Even so - still, though, although, yet, but

- Even though I love to travel, I just don't have the time

Worthwhile - for something to have been worth the effort or money: beneficial, excellent, justifiable

- The old Ferrari was really expensive, but it was worthwhile
- Studying English can be difficult, but it is worthwhile

Hardly - almost not at all: barely, almost not, rarely, seldom

- I have hardly any time to study English
- There are hardly any tickets left for the concert

Crushing - a very strong force pressing onto an object: push, press, mash

- The machine crushed the man!

Carried Away - to get excited, lose control: bewitched, captivated, intoxicated, possessed

- The dog gets so carried away when we go for a work

Surged - a big force pushing at once: flow, swell, rise, an outpouring

-
  The water surged over the wall
- The crowd surged towards the famous actor

Narrower - to be narrow if the opposite of wide: limited, constricted

-
  The road behind my house is narrow
- That river is much narrower than the Amazon

Fit into - to enter into a space

-
  The little dog can fit into very small spaces
- I can't fit any more food into me!

Breathing heavily - to breath in an intense way from exertion or strong physical activity

-
  The football player was breathing really heavily after running

Manage to - to be able to, achieve, to do something

-
  Did you manage to do your homework?

- I think I will manage to finish the project tomorrow

While - at the same time: whilst, simultaneously, concurrently

- Your friend is at the beach while you are reading this book
- I can brush my teeth while I dance

Get out of - to leave, escape

- We need to get out of this prison!
- Get out of my office before I call the police!

Although - comparative: even though, albeit, despite

- Although it is raining, I will still go out for a run
- I like pizza, although I prefer sushi if I have the choice

Afterwards - after a previous thing

- I have a meeting at 5 pm, but I can have a coffee with you afterwards

Whatever - Anything that happens: any, everything, whatsoever

-

Whatever you do, be careful
- You can eat whatever you like at the restaurant
- I thought to myself, whatever, it isn't important

Neither - not one nor the other

-

  Neither of the two friends went to the beach
- Me neither
- I want neither of them

Wherever - in any possible place

-

  Wherever you go in Italy, the food is always good
-

  We can meet for a coffee wherever is convenient for you
- I can go wherever I like in my car

Final words........

I hope that you found this book useful and that it has helped you to learn some new vocabulary and phrases in English. Remember, learning English can be frustrating and difficult, but it is so important in today's world. With better English you can go anywhere, do anything and talk to anybody you meet, English is the key to new possibilities and opportunities so continue studying and do not give up!

If this book helped your English then please take 2 minutes to write a positive reference for the book on Amazon. This will help the book to be more visible and help other English students find it in the future.

Thanks a lot, and good luck with your English studies!

Rhys

Printed in Great Britain
by Amazon